Sparkleton
The Mini Mistake

HARPER **Chapters**

Sparkleton
The Mini Mistake

BY CALLIOPE GLASS

ILLUSTRATED BY

HOLLIE MENGERT

HARPER

An Imprint of HarperCollinsPublishers

To Patty,

the meanest horse I ever loved.

Sparkleton #3: The Mini Mistake
Copyright © 2020 by HarperCollins Publishers
All rights reserved. Printed in Spain.
www.harperchapters.com
Library of Congress Control Number: 2020935525
ISBN 978-0-06-294798-7 — ISBN 978-0-06-294797-0 (paperback)
The artist used Photoshop to create the digital illustrations for this book.
Typography by Andrea Vandergrift
20 21 22 23 24   EP   10 9 8 7 6 5 4 3 2 1
❖
First Edition

TABLE OF CONTENTS

1: I Got *Wish-Granting* Magic!......................1

2: I Have to Practice First!........................9

3: Well, *This* Is New and Terrible!.............15

4: She's Beautiful!..................................23

5: I Don't Think You Can Fight a Hawk with

Confetti...31

6: SPLURCH! SPLURCH SPLURCH!.........38

7: I'm Not Sad. I'm Afraid.....................47

8: You're the Nicest Unicorn I've Ever Met....58

9: The Comedy Stylings of "TwinkleTon"!......69

10: Hey, Shimmer Lake!........................79

I Got Wish-Granting Magic!

Sparkleton was a small, shaggy purple unicorn. And more than anything, he wanted to have wish-granting magic. He wanted it so *much*. He wanted it *right now*. But everyone kept telling him to be patient.

There were many different kinds of unicorn magic, from confetti magic to invisibility.

Sparkleton only wanted wish-granting magic. And Sparkleton did *not* want to wait.

But now he'd finally found a way to make his magic come faster! No more waiting. No more wishing.

"All I have to do is stand on one hoof while yodeling," he explained to Willow and Gabe. "And then I'll get wish-granting magic right away!"

Willow and Gabe watched, eyes wide, as Sparkleton reared up. He staggered back and forth, trying to get his balance.

"Okay, I'm on two hooves!" he said. "Now I just have to lift one of my back hooves. I know I can do this!"

Concentrating hard, Sparkleton shifted all his weight to his right hind leg.

Carefully, carefully, he lifted his left hind hoof. It worked! He was balancing on one leg! Now all he had to do was yodel. He was so *close*!

Sparkleton took a deep breath, and—
"Sparkleton, for the last time, *wake up*!"
Huh?!

Sparkleton's eyes shot open. It had all been a dream! He'd fallen asleep in class . . . and now everyone was looking at him and laughing!

Sparkleton blushed so hard his face turned maroon. He was embarrassed!

"Are the seven hundred and ninety-three rules of proper unicorn spell casting *that* boring,

Sparkleton?" Gramma Una asked. Everyone snickered.

The answer, of course, was *yes*.

But Sparkleton knew he couldn't say that to Gramma Una's face.

"Of course not!" he told Gramma Una. He grinned at her and winked. "Someone must have put a sleeping spell on me!" He squeezed his eyes shut, flopped his ears down, and made a loud snoring noise. The whole class burst into laughter.

SNOOOORRRE!

It's fun when I'm making them laugh on purpose, Sparkleton thought. He pretended to wake up with a snort.

"It happened again!" he said. He shook his head. "Maybe it's pixies!"

Everyone laughed even harder.

Sparkleton was having so much fun! He jumped and yelped, "Ouch!" Then he turned and looked at his rear. "I think one of the pixies *bit* me!"

DALE

ROSIE

ZUZU

Rosie laughed so hard she snorted. Dale was giggling so much that he nearly fell over.

Sparkleton grinned. This was the most fun he'd had in weeks! He might not have wish-granting magic (yet), but at least he was still sparkletastic! And everyone else knew it!

And it's not like anyone else *has suddenly gotten wish-granting magic*, he thought. At least there was that.

"Everyone!" a voice called. "I got my magic!

I got *wish-granting* magic!"

The laughter stopped. All the unicorns, including Sparkleton, spun to look. A pink unicorn was trotting over the hill toward them.

"I got wish-granting magic!" she said again. She pranced happily.

Sparkleton felt like he'd swallowed a twenty-pound rock.

The happy unicorn was Twinkle.

2

I Have to Practice First!

Just a moment ago, Sparkleton had been the center of everyone's attention. His friends had been laughing and cheering. He'd been so happy. It had all been completely glitterrific.

Now he felt like sticking his head in a gopher hole.

Not only did he *still* not have magic, but now *Twinkle* had magic. Not only did *Twinkle* have magic . . . she had *wish-granting* magic.

It was *so unfair*.

Sparkleton had never really liked Twinkle. He didn't have a good reason, but that didn't stop him. She was just so . . . *nice*. So *kind*. She blinked a lot, and she never laughed at *anything* Sparkleton thought was funny.

And now she had wish-granting magic.

The whole class crowded around Twinkle, begging her to grant their wishes.

I wish I had bigger hooves!

I wish I could find one single goblin! Just one! Okay, maybe two.

I wish for a field full of clover!

I wish for a talking ladybug!

I wish you guys would quit yelling.

"I have to practice first!" Twinkle said. "Having wish-granting magic is a big responsibility! I want to treat my new powers with respect!"

Sparkleton snorted. That was the most boring thing he'd ever heard. If *he* had woken up with wish-granting powers, he'd be swimming in a lake full of singing glowworms by now.

"Well, I guess there's no way you foals are going to be able to concentrate on your lessons now," Gramma Una said. "Class is dismissed.

But before you all run off, take a look at this!"
She held up a big flyer.

TONIGHT!
SHIMMER LAKE TALENT SHOW!
NO MAGIC ALLOWED!!!
First Prize: 1 Pixie Cap!
Second Prize: 1 piece of goblin gold!
Third Prize: 1 clover ice-cream sundae!

The annual talent show! It was *tonight*? And first prize was a *Pixie Cap*?! Sparkleton forgot all about Twinkle. A Pixie Cap was a cute little hat that granted one glorious wish to the unicorn wearing it. He *had* to win it!

Plus, Sparkleton *loved* the talent show! Last year he'd sung a song about wishes while balancing on his horn.

Oh my glitter! Let's do something together!

Us three?

Yeah! Let's do a dance routine!

I'm going to make a daisy cake!

I have **NO IDEA** what I'm going to do!

Gabe looked worried. "Isn't goblin magic forbidden?" he asked.

"Forbidden, schmorbidden," Willow said.

"This is going to end in disaster," Gabe said gloomily.

Well, *This* Is New and Terrible!

Sparkleton, Willow, and Gabe went to Gabe's mushroom garden to plan for the talent show.

"I was thinking of entering my *Spotticus dotticus* in the talent show," Gabe said, nodding at one mushroom. "Or maybe this *yuckius* over here . . ."

Willow nodded attentively. But Sparkleton tuned him out. Gabe's mushrooms were *so boring*, and Sparkleton's head was spinning.

What a weird day. First he'd had that wonderful dream, then he'd made everyone laugh in class. Then Twinkle . . .

Ugh. He didn't even want to *think* about Twinkle.

And now the talent show was *tonight*! He needed an act. And it had to be *sparkletastic.*

Sparkleton had a plan. He was going to win the talent show, get the Pixie Cap, and grant his own wish for wish-granting magic. And then *everything would be glitterrific forever.*

"Sparkleton, are you even *listening*?" Gabe asked impatiently. He was pointing at a group of especially gross-looking mushrooms.

"Of course!" Sparkleton lied. "They're very pretty," he added.

That was also a lie.

Just then, something tickled Sparkleton's hoof. He looked down. A snail was sliming its way up his leg!

DON'T TOUCH!

"Ew!" Sparkleton said. He shook his hoof, but the snail stayed put. "Get it off!" Sparkleton told Gabe.

"Relax," Gabe said. "That's just my garden snail. I call her Booger."

"That doesn't really make me feel better," Sparkleton said. "Please make her go away." Booger wasn't very big—maybe the size of a mouse—but Sparkleton still wanted her to leave. She was getting slime on his fur.

Gabe talked quietly with Booger for a moment. The snail turned around and slimed her way back down Sparkleton's hoof and onto the dirt.

"So as I was saying," Gabe said, "before I was so *rudely* interrupted—" He frowned at Sparkleton.

"Hey," Sparkleton protested. "*Your snail* did the interrupting, not me!"

"It's not like you were paying attention anyway!" Gabe said. He was so annoyed that his ears had turned completely around. "I bet you couldn't even tell me which mushroom I was talking about."

Sparkleton rolled his eyes. "Of course I can."

He chose one at random. "You were talking about this one," he said, and poked it with his horn.

"*NO, DON'T TOUCH—*" Gabe cried.

But it was too late. The tip of Sparkleton's horn sank into the mushroom, and—

POOM!

Everything went white.

Then everything went black.

Sparkleton blinked and blinked, trying to clear the shimmers from his eyes.

When he could see again, he looked around. Nothing made sense. He was in a huge, dark space. And he was surrounded by giant mushrooms!

"Well, *this* is new and terrible!" said a cheerful voice behind him. Willow! Sparkleton turned. Gabe and Willow were there, too, looking around in surprise.

"Where *are* we?" Willow said. "This almost looks like Gabe's mushroom garden, except—"

"Except everything's *huge*," Sparkleton said. "Everything got *giant*."

"No," Gabe said gloomily. "We got small."

Oh my glitter! What do you think we'll do NOW?

4

She's Beautiful!

"**T**hat's what that mushroom *does*," Gabe explained sourly. The three friends were slowly making their way out of the garden. "It makes things tiny. That's why I have that warning sign in front of it. And *no*, I don't have a makes-things-bigger mushroom. There's no natural cure. I guess we're stuck like this. Forever."

"Don't be so dramatic. We'll just find a wish-granting unicorn to undo it," Willow said.

She rolled her eyes. "Sparkleton, doesn't Nella have a hangout nearby?" she asked. "We can find her and wish to be normal size again."

"Uh-huh," Sparkleton said. "Sure." He wove his way around mushrooms twice his height. He wasn't really listening to Willow and Gabe—he was too distracted. Being tiny was *shimmerrific*!

Everything was huge, and you could see all sorts of weird details. The gills under the mushrooms looked like the ripples on the water of Shimmer Lake. The nubs of dirt on the ground were like big, crumbly rocks. And everything smelled rich and strange. His nostrils flared. Then he smelled something new—something salty, like the sea.

"What—" Sparkleton started to say. But Willow interrupted him.

"Oh *wow*," she said. "*Oh, wow!* Hi, Booger!"

25

The salty smell was Booger.

The garden snail the size of a mouse was now almost as big as the unicorns.

"Huh," Sparkleton said. He tilted his head. "You know, now that I see her up close . . ."

She's beautiful!

She was! Even Sparkleton thought so. Booger's pearly shell shone with a thousand colors. Her body had faint polka dots all over it, and it gleamed in the dim light. Her feelers waved gracefully at them. She made a kind of quiet popping noise as she slimed her way along the ground.

"Wow," Willow whispered as Booger glided away.

The world outside the garden was even more sparkletastic. Now that they were small, everything was a cool new toy!

"Yahoooo!" Sparkleton yelled as he ran toward a fallen leaf. It was as big as his bed! He took a running jump and landed on it with his legs braced. The leaf slid along the moss just like a sled in wintertime!

YAHOOOO!

"Come see!" Willow called. She had gone a little farther into the meadow. "There are wild strawberries here in the grass!"

Soon Sparkleton, Willow, and Gabe were munching on enormous wild strawberries. Sparkleton had never tasted anything so delicious.

After their snack, Willow and Gabe started a game of kickball with an acorn. Sparkleton found an empty spider web and turned it into his own personal trampoline.

"Look at me!" he yelled as he bounced. He went higher and higher. Soon he was sailing above the tops of the high grass.

"Check this out!" he called to Willow and Gabe. He did a flip at the top of his next bounce.

"Yikes," Gabe said flatly. But Sparkleton could tell he was impressed.

On his next bounce, Sparkleton struck a pose as he reached the top. "I'm Nella!" he called. He scowled and shook his head. "*Sparkleton, quit bugging me!*" he said, imitating her slightly squeaky voice.

Then he tumbled back down to the spider web.

Willow giggled, and Gabe nearly cracked a smile.

Sparkleton decided to do Gramma Una next, but as he sailed up on his next bounce, a dark shadow slid across the sun.

A piercing *skree!* shattered the air.

"Hawk!!!" Gabe shrieked.

A hawk had spotted them! It was hungry . . .

And they were snack-size.

★ ★ ★ ⭐ ☆ ☆ ☆ ☆ ☆ ☆

5

I Don't Think You Can Fight a Hawk with Confetti

"*Run!*" Willow yelled.

Gabe made a break for a big blueberry bush. "We can hide in here!" he called as he ran. "It won't be able to reach us!"

High above them, the hawk moved into a dive. It got bigger and bigger as it rocketed toward them.

"*This* is why I need goblin magic!" Willow panted as they fled toward the blueberry bush.

"For emergencies!"

Sparkleton looked up as they ran. The hawk was a black shape that blotted out the whole sky. It was almost on top of them. They weren't going to make it in time.

He squeezed his eyes closed and *ran*.

"We made it!" Willow yelled. The three tiny unicorns slid under the thick branches and leaves of the bush and huddled by the trunk.

Crash!

The bush shook and trembled as the hawk smashed into it. The giant bird beat its huge wings and tore at the branches with razor-sharp claws, but the bush was too bushy! The hawk couldn't break through the branches.

The hawk flapped away, climbed into the air, and turned to dive again.

"Uh-oh," Gabe said.

Crash! It smashed into the blueberry bush again, screeching hungrily.

"We better do something," Willow said. "It knows we're in here. If it keeps doing this, it might actually get through the branches."

Gabe squared his shoulders. "I can use my magic," he said. "I'll take care of it."

Sparkleton tilted his head. "Yeah, but you've got confetti magic," he pointed out. "I don't think you can fight a hawk with confetti."

"No," Willow said thoughtfully. "You can't. But confetti magic includes all celebration magic. And that means . . ."

"*Fireworks*," Sparkleton said. Gabe nodded, and Sparkleton's eyes went wide. "Oh *sparkles*, this is going to be good."

The hawk had flown back into the sky and was beginning a third dive.

Gabe pointed his horn through the branches of the blueberry bush. He aimed at the hawk as it came toward them.

"*FireworksfireworksFIREWORKS!*" he cried. Yellow and blue fireworks erupted from his horn. Suddenly, the air above the blueberry bush was thundering and popping with blinding light! It was the biggest fireworks display Sparkleton had ever seen.

The hawk screeched again—but this time in terror. It skidded to a halt midair. Then it took off in the other direction.

The unicorns watched it go through the smoke and fading shimmer of the fireworks.

"We're safe," Sparkleton said. He let out a big, trembly breath.

"For now," Gabe agreed. "But we have to get back to normal size before something else tries to eat us."

"You know, instead of finding Nella, maybe we should try to contact goblins for help!" Willow said. "I've been reading about it, you guys, and I think if we say 'Shimmer Lake' backward three times while crossing our eyes—"

NO!!

Willow pouted.

"We've got to find Nella," Gabe said. "And we've got to do it without getting eaten."

You've read five chapters and 2,581 words. And you didn't even need GOBLIN MAGIC!

6

SPLURCH! SPLURCH SPLURCH!

S*critch.* A dark shape scurried past the three unicorns.

They all jumped. Sparkleton's heart nearly leapt out of his chest.

"What was that?" Willow gasped.

But it was just a mole hurrying through the blueberry bush. It trotted right past them without a second look.

"Phew," Sparkleton sighed.

"I nearly died of fright," Gabe wheezed. He put his head between his legs and took a few deep breaths.

"We really have to get somewhere safe," Willow said. "Before Gabe *actually* dies of fright."

Or before I do, Sparkleton thought. *I wish we could ask someone for advice. Like that mole—*

Wait, that was it!

"I've got it!" Sparkleton cried. "We can follow the mole! Moles live underground—and underground is *way* safer for a bunch of tiny unicorns than the meadow!"

"Brilliant, Sparkleton!" Willow cried. The three unicorns followed the mole to the edge of the blueberry bush.

And then the mole disappeared.

"What—" Sparkleton started. He hurried over . . . and discovered a hole. It was the perfect size for a tiny unicorn. "Here we go!" he said, and hopped right into it.

The tunnel was warm and dark and steep. Sparkleton, Willow, and Gabe scrambled a bit, trying to stay upright. But soon it leveled out. The dirt walls of the tunnel were packed smooth, so it was easy to follow. But it was also pitch dark. Until—

"Duh," Gabe said to himself.

"*SparklersparklerSPARKLER!*" and the tip of his horn lit up with tiny sparks. It was just enough light to show the tunnel around them. The mole was long gone, but at least now they could see.

"Good thinking, Gabe!" Sparkleton said. "Now we just have to keep on in this direction, and these tunnels should take us to Nella's corner of the meadow."

But going in one direction turned out to be impossible. The tunnels twisted and turned.

They split and dead-ended. And not all of them were empty.

"GAH!" Sparkleton shrieked as he turned down a branch of the tunnel and came face-to-face with a giant, slimy worm.

Behind him, Willow and Gabe both squeaked as well.

"Ugh!" Gabe said.

"Back up!" Willow yelled. "Back up, back up, back up!"

The worm wiggled a little and oozed slime along the wall of the tunnel. Sparkleton backed up so fast he almost fell head over hooves.

The three friends galloped down the other branch of the tunnel. After a while, they stopped, panting.

"Meeting that worm almost made me miss Booger," Sparkleton said. "At least Booger is *pretty*."

Willow laughed.

"Maybe we should find our way back up again," Gabe said.

"Do you think we're going in the right direction?" Willow asked.

Sparkleton shrugged. "I don't really care anymore," he admitted. "As long as we're going away from that worm. Did you see how gross it was?" He did a wiggly little wormy shimmy and made the grossest sliming noise he could manage.

SPLURCH! SPLURCH SPLURCH!

Willow and Gabe
cracked up.

Sparkleton
grinned and kept
a stream of jokes
going as he led his
friends through the
tunnel. And pretty
soon—

"Light!" Willow cried.

They had reached the far end of the meadow.

★ ★ ★ ★ ★ ⭐6 ☆ ☆ ☆ ☆

7

I'm Not Sad.
I'm Afraid.

Sparkleton, Willow, and Gabe scrambled up the tunnel and popped out into the fresh air.

"Phew," Gabe said. "That was too dark and too dank. And I *like* dark and dank."

"Yeah, I know," Sparkleton said. "I've been to your cave."

He looked around. No hawks. They were surrounded by high grass, but he could see the big old oak tree nearby.

Nella's secret spot was close to that tree. Soon they'd be back to their normal size. And then Sparkleton could start working on his act for the talent show so he could win the Pixie Cap.

"We're almost there," he said. He pointed his horn toward the pine. "Maybe we can just make a break for it—"

THA-DA-BOOM!

The ground shook violently. Sparkleton

scrambled to keep his balance, and Willow actually tumbled over.

Gabe helped her up. "What was *that*?!" he squeaked.

THA-DA-BOOM!

THA-DA-BOOM!

The ground heaved and trembled. Was it an earthquake? A volcano? Was Shimmer Lake being attacked by goblins?

And then the screaming started. Great, deep voices were howling in rhythm.

It almost sounded like . . .

"Is that *singing*?" Willow said, her eyes wide.

"Yeah, I think it's—*run!*" Gabe yelled.

Three mountain-size unicorns thundered toward them. Their hoofbeats struck in time with each other. They were singing in earsplitting voices. It was the most horrible thing Sparkleton had ever seen—or heard.

"And walk-two-three and trot-two-three," one of the giant unicorns said. Her voice sounded like a thousand rocks breaking at once. "Then turn, and rear up."

Suddenly, Sparkleton understood what was happening.

The huge unicorns were Britta, Zuzu, and Rosie. And they were practicing their song-and-dance routine for the talent show. If Sparkleton and his friends weren't careful, they were going to get trampled in the dance.

Sparkleton, Gabe, and Willow hightailed it away from them. Sparkleton wasn't paying any attention to where they were going—he only knew they had to get away before they got stomped or went deaf—or both.

Finally, with the dancing unicorns well behind them, the three tiny friends slid to a halt. They were panting and worn out. And Sparkleton had no idea where they were.

And then they heard it. A unicorn was crying.

But who was it? And where were they? Sparkleton looked around. If he could find another spider web trampoline, maybe he could bounce high enough to see. Then Gabe pointed with his horn—"There!" he said.

They scrambled up the trunk of a nearby tree, using some shelf fungus as stairs. And once the three tiny unicorns were high enough, they could see who was crying—

"It's *Twinkle*," Sparkleton gasped. The pink unicorn was all by herself in a clump of ferns. She was crying as quietly as she could. But to the ears of the tiny unicorns, it was as loud as a raging river.

The three friends scrambled down the tree and galloped over to their classmate. Huge tears rolled down her nose and splashed onto the ground. Sparkleton dodged one right before it hit him.

"Twinkle!" Willow yelled at the top of her lungs. "Twinkle! Down here!"

Gabe joined in, then Sparkleton did, too. The three friends yelled as loudly as they could.

At first, nothing happened. Then Twinkle sniffled. She opened her eyes. She looked around, confused.

"TWINKLE!" Sparkleton, Willow, and Gabe all yelled. And she looked right at them.

"Sprinkles and sparkles!" Twinkle gasped.

She seemed to have forgotten all about whatever was making her so sad. "What *happened* to you guys?!"

"What happened to *you*?" Gabe demanded. "I've never seen you cry before. You're always so—so—"

So cheerful!

So annoying.

"I'm not sad," Twinkle said. She sniffled again. Her breath shuddered a little in her chest. "I'm afraid."

Sparkleton was so, so confused. "Of *what*?" he asked. Twinkle was never afraid of anything.

Twinkle squeezed her eyes shut. "Of the talent show."

More than halfway through! You must be as DETERMINED as Sparkleton!

8

You're the Nicest Unicorn
I've Ever Met

Twinkle had *stage fright*?!

Sparkleton had never been so confused in his whole entire life. Twinkle was the most confident unicorn he knew. She was *annoyingly* confident. Plus, everyone loved her! Well, everyone except Sparkleton. How could she have stage fright? He didn't understand it. And he wanted to.

Sparkleton found himself hating Twinkle a

little less—it was hard not to like someone you wanted to understand better.

"Can you explain—" Sparkleton started. But Twinkle brushed away his questions. "Forget about me," she said, shaking her head. "We have to get *you* guys fixed up! Here, make a wish! I'll get you back to normal in no time."

"Okay," Willow said. "I wish we were all back to our usual size."

Twinkle began the wish spell. First, she stamped her front hooves: left, then right.

Then she lowered her nose to the ground and snorted three times.

Finally, she carefully traced a circle in the air with the tip of her horn. It began to glow. Twinkle looked deep into Willow's eyes. Willow stared back at her. For a long moment, neither of them blinked. Then—

"Thy wish is granted," Twinkle said. She tapped Willow on the nose with her horn.

BOOP!

Suddenly, Sparkleton, Willow, and Gabe were—

Even tinier?!

"Whoa!" Sparkleton yelled. His voice sounded like an angry ladybug. A huge shape cast a shadow over him, and he jumped, frightened. It was a firefly!

Sparkleton let out a big, relieved sigh. Fireflies were harmless. But this one was definitely on its way to the talent show to help light the stage. And that meant time was running out.

"I'm so sorry!" Twinkle said in horror. "I did a circle instead of a figure eight! I messed up the spell!"

"Do it again," Gabe said. His voice sounded like a cricket. "I wish we were all our normal size again!"

Twinkle did the spell again, and this time she traced a figure eight instead of a circle. Then she very, very carefully tapped Gabe with her horn. It still almost knocked him over.

"Thy wish is granted," Twinkle said in a voice like a thousand elephants yelling.

PING!

Now they were the size of trees! *Big* trees! Sparkleton peered down at Twinkle. Suddenly, she looked like she was the size of a mouse.

"*Yikes!*" Twinkle said. Her voice sounded small and squeaky to Sparkleton's giant ears.

She raised her horn and tried one more time.

This time Sparkleton made the wish.

POOM!

Sparkleton, Willow, and Gabe were *finally back to normal*. Sparkleton was so relieved that he almost wasn't mad anymore that Twinkle had wish-granting powers and he still didn't. He *almost* wasn't mad. But not quite.

"Phew!" Twinkle said. "That's a relief. See,

this is why I didn't want to grant everyone a wish this morning. I'm still learning!"

"Sure, sure," Sparkleton said impatiently. "You're *so* responsible. We know. But why are you afraid of the talent show, Twinkle?"

Twinkle stamped one hoof uncomfortably. She looked down. "I don't know." She sighed. "I guess . . . I love helping others. That's why I've always wanted wish-granting magic. And now I have it, which is so amazing! But I can't use it at the talent show. And the thing is . . . I don't actually have any talents." Twinkle sighed again. "There's just nothing special about me."

Sparkleton turned to stare at Willow and Gabe. They seemed as amazed as he was.

"Listen," Sparkleton told Twinkle. "This is hard for me to say. This might be the hardest thing I've ever said. But . . ." He took a deep breath. "You are special, Twinkle," he said. "You're *annoyingly* special. You're so special that it kind of makes me want to barf. You sing fireflies to sleep every morning. You tuck caterpillars

into their cocoons at night. You know the birthday of every single unicorn in Shimmer Lake. You're the nicest unicorn I've ever met. And that makes you incredibly annoying, but it also makes you veryveryveryvery*very* special."

Twinkle looked at him with wide eyes.

Sparkleton sighed. "And I don't have an act for the talent show, either," he admitted.

Twinkle's eyes got even wider.

Stop talking, Sparkleton told himself. *Stop talking right now.* But it was as though his brain and his mouth weren't connected.

"Maybe . . ." Sparkleton started. *Oh great glitter and glimmer, don't do this, Sparkleton*, he thought. "Maybe we can team up for the talent show."

The Comedy Stylings of "TwinkleTon"!

Twinkle blinked. Once, twice. And then she smiled the sunniest, happiest smile.

"Yes!" she said. "Thank you, Sparkleton. You're always so nice to me!"

"I'm really not," Sparkleton said. "Mostly I'm super mean to you."

"You're the *best*," Twinkle said. She bumped his shoulder with her shoulder in a unicorn hug.

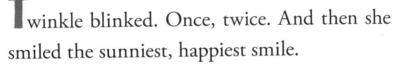

69

"No, I'm really, really—"

"Just let it go, Sparkleton," Willow said.

"Okay," Sparkleton said. "Fine. I'm the best."

"So, what should we do for the talent show?" Twinkle asked.

Sparkleton flicked his ears in a unicorn shrug. "I have no idea," he said. And that worried him. He needed to win the talent show . . . so he could get that Pixie Cap and finally get wish-granting magic!

Willow frowned. "Let's see," she said thoughtfully, "Rosie, Britta, and Zuzu are doing a song-and-dance routine . . ."

"We could give everyone earplugs," Sparkleton joked, remembering how awful their singing had sounded when he was tiny. "We might get first prize just for that."

Gabe glared at Sparkleton. "That's not very nice," he said disapprovingly.

Willow tried hard not to laugh.

Then—to everyone's surprise—Twinkle giggled.

"That was a mean thing to say," she said. "But it was funny, too. Sparkleton, you're always so funny."

Sparkleton beamed. He was really starting to like Twinkle all of a sudden.

"It's true," Willow said. "He is funny. Remember that whole thing where he was pretending to fall asleep in class this morning?"

Gabe snickered. "And the impression of Nella he did on the spider web trampoline?"

"And the SPLURCH sound he made when we were in the mole tunnel?" Willow added.

Twinkle gasped. "That's it!" she said. "I've got it! Sparkleton is so good at being funny . . . We should do a *comedy* routine for the talent show!"

Sparkleton's eyes went wide. "That could be really good, Twinkle!" he said.

Maybe he would win that Pixie Cap after all!

"We have to hurry to the talent show!" Willow said. "It's starting soon! We can get Gabe's mushroom on our way."

"And we can plan our comedy routine!" Twinkle told Sparkleton.

They all hurried toward the beach.

When they arrived, the sun was setting over Shimmer Lake. All the unicorns had gathered on the beach. They'd set up a big stage made of driftwood and seaweed. Thousands of fireflies hovered over it, shining down on the stage.

Sparkleton wondered which of them was the firefly he'd seen when he was small.

"First up!" called Gramma Una. "Rosie, Zuzu, and Britta."

The three young unicorns trotted onto the stage for their song-and-dance routine. Their singing actually sounded pretty good to Sparkleton, now that he was back at his normal size.

After them was
Nella, who juggled
pinecones with her
nose.

Privately, Sparkleton
thought it was kind of
silly. But he stomped
his hooves in unicorn applause when she was
done. She was his sister, after all.

Next, Dale brought out his daisy cake, and
just seeing it made Sparkleton hungry.

But then Gabe presented a stinky, slimy mushroom, and after *that*, Sparkleton wasn't hungry anymore.

Gabe trotted off the stage with his mushroom. Willow was up next.

"For my act," Willow said, "I have prepared a goblin magic spell. Now, I know it's forbidden, but personally I think that's a very silly rule. Also, I should mention that I've never tried this before, but I'm *pretty* sure it's *pretty* safe—"

"Nope!" Gramma Una said as she whisked Willow offstage.

"*Next!*" Gramma Una cried. "We have the comedy stylings of 'TwinkleTon'!"

Sparkleton glanced over at Twinkle. She seemed a little nervous, but nothing worse than that. "Are you ready?" he asked. She nodded and smiled. Sparkleton smiled back. It was weird, being partners with Twinkle. He had kind of hated her forever. But this whole strange adventure had made him see her in a different light. Suddenly, her sweetness wasn't so annoying. It was just . . . sweet.

Sparkleton was almost *glad* he was doing the talent show with Twinkle. Weird.

"Let's do this," Sparkleton said. And they walked onto the stage.

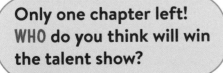

Only one chapter left!
WHO do you think will win
the talent show?

10

Hey, Shimmer Lake!

"**H**ey, Twinkle," said Sparkleton. He spoke loudly so that all the unicorns watching the talent show could hear him.

"Yes, Sparkleton?" Twinkle replied, just as loudly.

"Can a unicorn jump higher than an oak tree?" Sparkleton asked.

"Of course!" Twinkle said. "An oak tree can't jump!"

A few unicorns in the audience whinnied in unicorn laughter.

"Hey, Sparkleton," Twinkle said.

"Yes, Twinkle?" replied Sparkleton.

"How long should a unicorn's legs be?"

Sparkleton looked down at his short, stubby legs. Then he looked back up at Twinkle. "Long enough to touch the ground!" he said.

This time, a whole bunch of unicorns whinnied. Sparkleton grinned at Twinkle. This was going great!

"Hey, Twinkle," Sparkleton said.

"Yes, Sparkleton?" Twinkle replied.

"What do you call the unicorn next door?"

"Your *neigh*bor!" Twinkle replied, grinning.

The whole crowd whinnied and stomped their hooves in unicorn applause.

Sparkleton and Twinkle looked at each other and nodded. It was time to finish big.

"Hey, Shimmer Lake!" they said in unison, looking out at the crowd.

"Yes?" all the unicorns yelled back.

"What do you call a group of unicorns?" Sparkleton and Twinkle said in unison.

"What?" all the unicorns cried—even louder this time.

"A *neigh*borhood!" Sparkleton and Twinkle said.

The crowd erupted in whinnies of laughter. Sparkleton and Twinkle bowed and bowed.

"Sorry for being so *corny,* uni*corns,*" Sparkleton called as they left the stage. The crowd laughed even louder.

Sparkleton's heart was beating fast. He hadn't thought it would go this well! But Twinkle had been pretty good! And obviously, he'd been great.

Gramma Una stepped out onto the stage. The thousands of fireflies turned their lights up all the way. She smiled out at everyone.

"What a talented bunch!" she said. "But the judges have spoken, and the *most* talented unicorns in this year's talent show are . . ."

Sparkleton held his breath. The Pixie Cap was *about to be his*! Soon he would be a wish-granting unicorn! It was all coming together!

". . . Britta, Rosie, and Zuzu!" Gramma Una finished.

Britta, Rosie, and Zuzu shrieked happily and galloped onto the stage to accept their prize.

Sparkleton slumped. No Pixie Cap for him. Back to the drawing board.

Second place went to Gabe, but Gabe immediately marched off the stage and gave the goblin gold to Willow.

"I'm scared of that stuff," he said. "And I hated being up on that stage anyway."

Willow grinned. "I'll put it to good use," she promised.

"Please don't," Gabe begged.

Gramma Una cleared her throat.

"And third place goes to . . ."

But Sparkleton wasn't really listening anymore. He'd wanted that Pixie Cap *so badly*. He sighed. Another great idea down the drain.

Then Twinkle poked him with her horn.

"Huh?" he said.

"Sparkleton!" she said, prancing happily. "We won third place! Didn't you hear Gramma Una?"

Sparkleton felt dazed. "We did?" he said as Twinkle herded him onto the stage.

Twinkle grinned at him. "We did!" she said. "You're the best friend ever, Sparkleton." She bumped his shoulder in a unicorn hug.

"I am?" Sparkleton said, still feeling kind of stunned. Then he came back to himself. "I am!" he agreed.

He was *twinkletastic*.

And he was going to get his hands on that Pixie Cap somehow . . .

But first he was going to eat a clover ice-cream sundae with his friend Twinkle.

CALLIOPE GLASS is a writer and editor. She lives in New York City with two small humans and one big human, and a hardworking family of house spiders who are all named Gwen. There are no unicorns in her apartment, but they are always welcome.

HOLLIE MENGERT is an illustrator and animator living in Los Angeles. She loves drawing animals, making people smile with her work, and spending time with her amazingly supportive family and friends.

UNICORN GAMES

THINK!

Imagine you have shrunk down to the size of a mouse. What is the first thing you would do? Draw a picture of mini you having the best time ever with your mini friends.

FEEL!

Think of a time when you were afraid to do something. What did your friends say to get you excited to try something scary?

ACT!

What would you do for a talent show? Practice your routine and perform it for your family or closest friends!